Little Bunny
On the Move

To my wife and best friend,
Yunhee,
And our daughter,
Suki

Henry Holt and Company, LLC, *Publishers since 1866*
175 Fifth Avenue, New York, New York 10010
www.HenryHoltKids.com

Henry Holt is a registered trademark of Henry Holt and Company, LLC
Copyright © 1999 by Peter McCarty
All rights reserved.
Distributed in Canada by H. B. Fenn and Company Ltd.

Library of Congress Cataloging-in-Publication Data
McCarty, Peter. Little bunny on the move / by Peter McCarty.
Summary: A little bunny rabbit hurries past five fat sheep, over train tracks,
and across an open field on his way to a special destination.
[1. Rabbits—Fiction. 2. Home—Fiction.] I. Title.
PZ7.M47841327Li 1999 [E]—dc21 98-29787

ISBN 978-0-8050-4620-5 (hardcover)
5 7 9 10 8 6 4

ISBN 978-0-8050-7259-4 (paperback)
3 5 7 9 10 8 6 4
First published in hardcover in 1999 by Henry Holt and Company
First Owlet paperback edition, 2003
Printed in December 2010 in China by South China Printing Company Ltd.,
Dongguan City, Guangdong Province

The artist used pencils and watercolor on 140-pound watercolor paper
to create the illustrations for this book.

Little Bunny On the Move

WRITTEN AND ILLUSTRATED BY

Peter McCarty

HENRY HOLT AND COMPANY
NEW YORK

It was time for a little bunny
to be on the move.
From here to there,
a bunny goes where a bunny must.

Bunny, Bunny going down the path,
Bunny, Bunny, aren't you turning back?

Where are you going, Little Bunny?

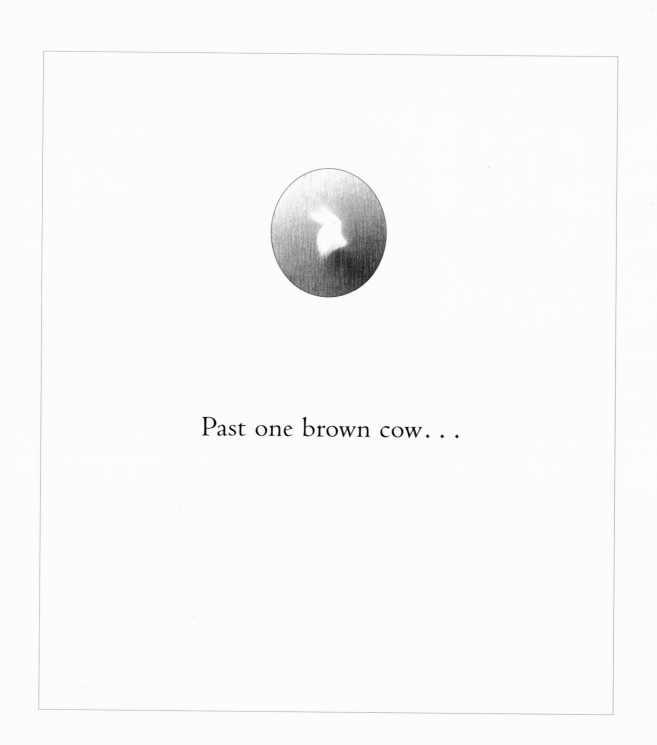

Past one brown cow. . .

past five fat sheep. . .

this bunny would not stop.

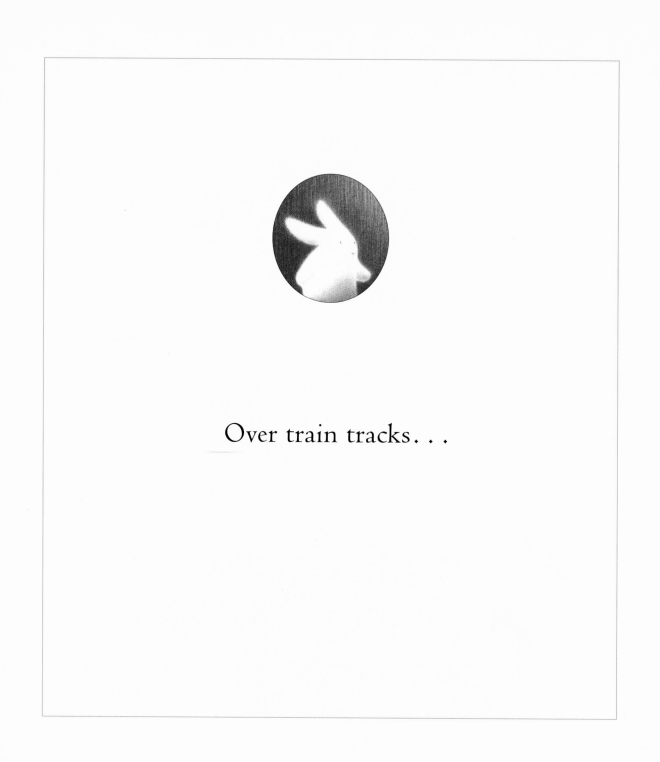

Over train tracks. . .

through a fence.

This bunny could not stop.
This bunny had a place to go.

Bunny, Bunny, the sky is turning black.

Bunny, Bunny, aren't you going back?

Won't you stop to sleep, Little Bunny?

"Hello, Little Bunny, hello!"

A voice wakes the sleeping bunny.

"Do you need a place to stay?
Do you need a home?"

"No thank you, not today!"

This bunny would not
be someone's pet.
This bunny would not stay.

Through the trees. . .

across an open field.

This bunny would not look back.
This bunny had come a long way.

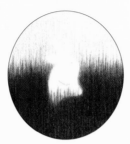

Bunny, Bunny going up the hill,
Bunny, Bunny, can you not sit still?
Where are you going, Little Bunny?

"Here, I'm going here.

You see, I have a home."

And this bunny did have a home.
This bunny did have a place to stay.